Casper Club

This book belongs to...

_____

Troublesome Sister

Bright ☆ Sparks

This is a Bright Sparks Book
First published in 2000
BRIGHT SPARKS, Queen Street House, 4 Queen Street, Bath BA1 1HE, UK

Copyright © PARRAGON 2000

Created and produced by THE COMPLETE WORKS,
St. Mary's Road, Royal Leamington Spa, Warwickshire CV31 1JP, UK

Editorial Director: Mike Phipps
Project Manager: Stuart Branch
Editor: Aneurin Rhys
Designer: Anne Matthews

Printed in Spain

ISBN 1-84250-007-4

ALLEY DOGS

Troublesome Sister

Written by Lesley Rees and Aneurin Rhys
Illustrated by Terry Burton

Bright ☆ Sparks

In the higgledy-piggledy, messy alley it was *tidy up time*! Harvey and the gang had worked hard all morning, scribbling and scrabbling in the heaps of junk trying to clean up their home.

At last, the skip was full of rubbish and they could have a break.

All the gang settled down for a snooze, except for Puddles, Harvey's little sister.

"Where's my teddy?" she wondered. "And where's my ish?" Puddles' 'ish' was a blanket she'd had since she was a baby.

It was full of holes and rather smelly, but she loved it lots.

She looked round the alley. "Teddy! Ish!" she called. "Where are you?" She didn't see them peeping out from the top of the skip.

Puddles was always getting into lots of mischief and today she scampered off down the alley, sure that she would find her teddy and ish down there somewhere. Spotting a hole in the fence, she peeped through and saw an old box of toys. "Are teddy and ish in there?" she wondered.

She squeezed and squashed herself through the gap and crept up to the toybox.

"Teddy! Ish! Are you in there?" she called. But they weren't. She did find an old toy mouse, hidden away at the back. "Doesn't anyone love you?" she asked. "You're very soft and cuddly – I'll love you!"

"Come on, Mousey," she giggled. "You come home with me." Puddles was feeling much happier.

But Lulu the kitten wasn't. The mouse was her favourite toy and as Puddles trotted off she began to wail.

"Mummy! Mummy! Come quickly!" she cried.

Hattie, Lulu's mum, appeared through a gap in the fence. "What a terrible noise you're making," she purred. "What is the matter?"

Lulu sobbed and sniffed. "Puddles has taken my Mousey!" cried the kitten.

"There, there," purred Hattie, trying to stop the sobs. "Don't you worry, Lulu, we'll soon get Mousey back."

But Lulu just screamed even louder.

Puddles didn't hear poor Lulu crying. She was dancing around the garden with her new friend. "We are having fun, aren't we, Mousey!" she laughed as she skipped along. "Now all I need is an ish."

As she skipped through the garden next door, Puddles saw a tatty, old scarf hanging down from the branch of an apple tree. "Oh look, Mousey!" she cried. "A cuddly ish with no one to love it."

"Well, it's not really an ish," she thought, "but it is very, very soft." She reached up and took one end in her mouth. With a pull and a tug, the scarf floated down. Puddles picked it up and cuddled it. Now she was really happy. She didn't see Lenny, Lulu's brother, fast asleep in the flowerbed.

Lenny woke up with a start and suddenly saw Puddles skipping off along the garden with his favourite scarf — the one he had hung in the tree to use as a swing! He couldn't believe his eyes and began to cry. "Mummy! Mummy!" he wailed.

Hattie and Lulu squeezed through the hedge.

"That naughty Puddles has stolen my scarf," sobbed Lenny.

Hattie sighed. Oh dear, now both her twins were crying.
Something would have to be done about that pup!

Puddles popped through the hedge and ran straight into—
the angry Alley Cats.

"Oh no!" gulped Puddles. "Someone's in trouble, and I
think it's *me*!"

Lulu and Lenny were hiding behind Hattie who looked very cross. Puddles was suddenly scared and she began to cry. "H-H-Harvey!" she croaked. "Help me!"

Puddles' wailing woke up Harvey and the gang.

"Is that Puddles I can hear?" said Ruffles. "Yes! Run, Harvey, *run*! Puddles needs your help!"

"Hang on, Puddles," woofed Harvey. "I'm coming!"

And off he ran, as fast as he could go...

Harvey burst through the hedge.
"Okay, guys!" he gasped.
"What's all the fuss about?"

The angry Alley Cats began shouting all at once.

Puddles hid behind her big brother and shivered and shook. Whatever had she done?

There was so much noise that Harvey couldn't hear what anyone was saying.

"QUIET!" he barked. And they were – even the kittens!

"Thank you," said Harvey. "Now then, Hattie, what is all the noise about?"

"That scally wag sister of yours has stolen my twins' favourite toys," grumbled Hattie.

"Did you, Puddles?" asked Harvey, sternly.

"I didn't mean to, Harvey," she cried. "I thought that no one wanted them."

She gave back little Mousey and the tattered and torn scarf. "Sorry, Lulu," she whimpered. "Sorry, Lenny. I only wanted to love them."

"That's okay, Puddles," smiled the twins. "But you see, we love them — lots and lots."

Hattie looked at Puddles and shook her head, she really was an annoying puppy. Harvey gave a huge sigh — panic over!

"Puddles, you're such a scamp," smiled Harvey.

"But I was only looking for my teddy and my ish," cried Puddles. "I don't know where they are."

"Oh, is that what this is all about?" said Harvey.

He scooped them from the skip and gave them back to Puddles with a hug and a kiss. "Now, no more trouble today," he said. "Let's all have a dog-nap. Okay?"

Puddles hugged her teddy and stroked her ish; she was happy again. "Well," said Puddles, looking at Harvey with a naughty grin, "ish and I will be good, but teddy might not!"

The End

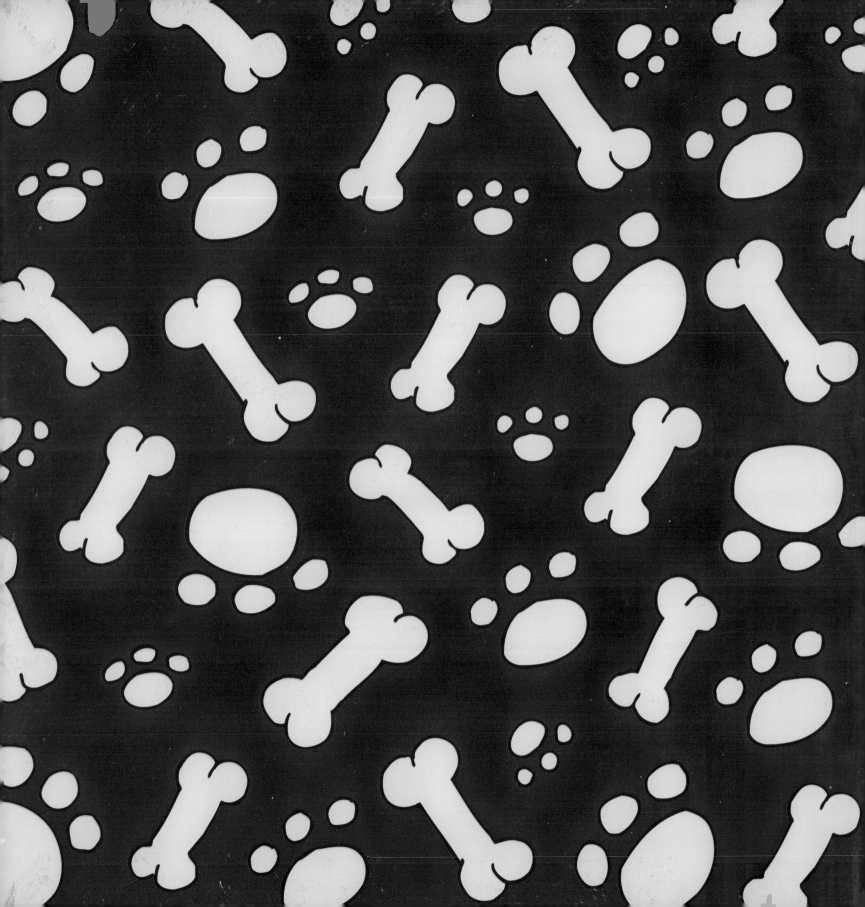